DOVER
CHILDREN'S THRIFT CLASSICS

W9-BSE-815

The Story of Pocahontas

BRIAN DOHERTY

Illustrated by Thea Kliros

DOVER PUBLICATIONS, INC.
New York

Copyright

Copyright © 1994 by Dover Publications, Inc.
All rights reserved under Pan American and International Copyright Conventions.

Published in Canada by General Publishing Company, Ltd., 30 Lesmill Road, Don Mills, Toronto, Ontario.
Published in the United Kingdom by Constable and Company, Ltd., 3 The Lanchesters, 162–164 Fulham Palace Road, London W6 9ER.

Bibliographical Note

The Story of Pocahontas is a new work, first published by Dover Publications, Inc., in 1994.

Library of Congress Cataloging-in-Publication Data

Doherty, Brian.
    The story of Pocahontas / Brian Doherty ; illustrated by Thea Kliros.
        p.   cm. — (Dover children's thrift classics)
    Summary: A fictionalized account of the life of Pocahontas who befriended Captain John Smith and the English settlers of Jamestown.
    ISBN 0-486-28025-X (pbk.)
    1. Pocahontas, d. 1617—Juvenile fiction. [1. Pocahontas, d. 1617—Fiction. 2. Powhatan Indians—Fiction. 3. Indians of North America—Fiction. 4. America—Discovery and exploration—English—Fiction.] I. Kliros, Thea, ill. II. Title. III. Series.
Z7.D6948St 1994
[Fic]—dc20
                                  94-27378
                                       CIP
                                       AC

Manufactured in the United States of America
Dover Publications, Inc., 31 East 2nd Street, Mineola, N.Y. 11501

Note

Although Pocahontas' is one of the most familiar names in American history, relatively little is known about her life apart from a few sparse details. Born around 1595 in the area now known as Jamestown, Pocahontas was the daughter of the powerful Indian leader Powhatan. The most famous event of her life was recorded in Captain John Smith's *Generall historie of Virginia:* captured by the Powhatan Indians, Smith was rescued by Pocahontas, who interceded with her father just as Smith was about to be executed. In 1613, Pocahontas was held hostage by the English in Jamestown until a temporary truce between the warring settlers and Indians could be arranged. A permanent peace (except for an outbreak in hostilities in 1622) was achieved in 1614 with the marriage of Pocahontas to John Rolfe. Pocahontas traveled to England in 1616 and died there of smallpox in 1617; she had one child, Thomas Rolfe, who was educated in England and later emigrated to Virginia.

Drawn from these facts, *The Story of Pocahontas* brings the Indian princess to life. Children will enjoy reading about her courage and heroism and her adventures during the early years of America's settlement.

Contents

List of Illustrations

Chapter 1

The English Arrive in Virginia

IN THE WINTER of 1606, three English ships, the *Susan Constant*, the *Godspeed* and the *Discovery*, started across the Atlantic under the command of Captain Christopher Newport. They carried 105 men, intending to settle at Roanoke Island, where an English colony had disappeared twenty years before, but they were driven further north by a storm. After many months at sea, they began hunting for a suitable place for settlement. They sailed into the broad opening of Chesapeake Bay and were still moving northward when they encountered a wide river that flowed into the bay from the mainland on the west. They turned the prows of their ships into this river, which they called the James, in honor of their king, and studied the shores for an inviting spot to land.

It was May, with mild skies and soft breezes that kept the craft sailing against the current. These men, standing on their decks, were sure they had never gazed upon anything so beautiful. The banks were filled with wild flowers, whose fragrance wafted across the smooth waters, while the hills and mountains in the distance were softened to delicate tints against the blue sky.

There were men and women in this land, descendants of those who had lived there for unknown ages. They were standing on the shore, watching the approaching vessels. One party, among whom several women could be seen, stood at least a hundred yards back from the stream as if afraid to come nearer. Another party gathered on the edge of the river, where there was a natural clearing of an acre or two. When the *Susan Constant*, which was a hundred yards ahead of the smaller boats, pulled up alongside this group, two of the warriors on the bank let their arrows fly.

The men on the decks smiled at these efforts. Captain Newport suggested they fire their guns into the party, as they had done days before when greeted with a shower of arrows.

"No, we should cultivate their good will. We will need their friendship, and must not use our guns as long as our lives can be saved without them."

This remark was made by a man standing at the prow, spyglass in hand. He was of sturdy build, in well-to-do civilian's clothing, with a full sandy beard and a huge mustache. His face was deeply tanned, he wore a sword at his side and his face was resolute and firm. He was not yet thirty years of age and no one could look at his figure without seeing he had unusual strength. Mentally and physically, he was stronger than the officers and crew around him. This man was Captain John Smith, whose great services later earned him the name "Father of Virginia." He was one of the bravest of men—unselfish, enterprising and far-seeing.

By the afternoon of the next day, the three vessels had already traveled eighty miles from the mouth of the James River. They were approaching a peninsula where they had decided to make camp, when everyone's attention was turned upstream. Captain Smith lifted his telescope to his eyes. Around a bend in the river a canoe shot into sight.

Captain Newport, who also had a spyglass, stood near Smith and studied the small craft as well.

"Those two warriors have more courage than their friends," Newport remarked.

"There is only one warrior in the canoe," replied Smith, gazing through his telescope; "the other is a woman, and——"

Here Smith hesitated, but Newport spent another minute studying the canoe and said, "You are right—and the woman is not an old one."

"She is not a woman, but a girl."

Seated in the middle of the canoe was an Indian youth who was less than twenty years old. Propelling the boat, he faced the vessels downriver. He had long, black hair that dangled about his shoulders, and his face was stained with the juice of the *puccoon*, or bloodroot. His chest was bare but his waist was clasped with a deerskin girdle, a skirt falling below his knees, with leggings that reached to his neatly fitted beaded moccasins. He was finely formed, fleet-footed and a strong warrior despite his youth.

The other occupant of the little craft was the youth's sister. She was no more than twelve years old, with features of almost classical beauty. She had thrown back her doeskin robe, lined with wood dove's down. She wore coral bracelets on her wrists and ankles, and a white plume in her abundant hair.

Her leggings and skirt were similar to her brother's, but the upper part of her body was clothed in a close-fitting doeskin jacket that covered her arms to the elbow. Her face was not treated with the red juice that her brother used. This girl was a natural athlete who could speed through the woods like a deer, shoot an arrow with the accuracy of a veteran warrior, swim like a fish and read nature's faint signs the way we might read a book.

Nantaquas, as the young man was called, and his sister, Pocahontas, had left their home a long way up the river, paddling downstream, perhaps to call on some friends, when, rounding a bend in the river, they were startled by the sight of the three ships slowly coming up the river with their white sails spread. Nantaquas stopped paddling for a moment while both gazed at the sight. They had heard stories told by the tribes to the south of a people who lived far beyond the sea, with canoes like giant birds that were able to sail through storms in safety.

When Pocahontas had looked for several minutes in silent amazement at the European ships, watching the men on the decks, she asked:

"Why are they coming to the country of Powhatan?"

"I don't know," her brother replied, "maybe they intend to take away our hunting grounds."

"How can that be," the girl laughed, "when the warriors of Powhatan are like the leaves on the trees? There are only a handful of the white folk—we have nothing to fear from them. Let's visit the big canoes."

The youth increased the speed of his boat, drawing rapidly near the *Susan Constant*, whose passengers and crew watched his approach with keen curiosity. Nantaquas sped on downstream, however, doubting the wisdom of carrying out his sister's wishes. She believed that any people who were treated kindly would give the same treatment to those that were good to them.

But Nantaquas recalled that the stories of the white men he had heard were not to their credit. Some of them had slain Indians as though they were wild animals; they had treated them with great cruelty and repaid kindness with brutality. The tribes along the coasts further south told of the Spanish explorers who came looking for gold and a Fountain of Youth, bringing with them sickness and war. Many Indians had been killed or taken from their homelands as slaves. Closer to the land of Powhatan there had been other Englishmen, too. But their settlement on Roanoke Island and all the white people there had mysteriously disappeared almost twenty years ago, before Nantaquas was born.

Whether they were killed by the Indians, or whether they had joined the friendly tribes who perhaps rescued them from starvation, Nantaquas was not sure. He realized, however, that too little was known about these new arrivals. They might be friendly, but they might just as likely try to carry off his sister or him as prisoners, or demand a high price for their ransom.

Nantaquas checked his boat a hundred yards from the largest vessel. Smith and the other passengers were at the rail of the *Susan Constant*, looking down at the visitors who hesitated to draw nearer.

"Welcome! Welcome!" Smith called out, "Won't you come aboard that we may shake hands and break bread with you?"

Although Nantaquas and his sister did not understand the words, the gestures of the men were clear.

"Why do you hesitate?" Pocahontas asked impatiently. "They want to greet us—don't be ungrateful."

But Nantaquas was decisive: "They are strangers—we have heard evil things of many of them. We shall go no closer."

In answer to the Englishmen's inviting gestures, Nantaquas raised one hand and waved

Nantaquas raised one hand and waved it toward the
ship.

it toward the ship. He meant it as a polite refusal to accept the invitation. Then he sent the canoe skimming upstream.

Smith noticed a strange thing at this point. Nothing seemed to escape his keen eyes. He saw a thin column of smoke filtering upward from among the trees on a wooded elevation, a little way inland. It had a wavy motion from side to side. The column of smoke was broken, showing two distinct gaps between the base and the top. There could be no question that it was a signal fire. He was certain that, whatever the message might be, it had to do with the Englishmen who were sailing up the great river, searching for a spot upon which to found their settlement.

Chapter 2

Pocahontas and Her Family

NANTAQUAS PADDLED like one who could never tire. He had come a long distance downstream on this day in May. His sister was displeased because of his refusal to take her aboard the big canoe and she meant him to know it. He understood her feeling, and wisely gave her time to get over it. Nevertheless, she was planning her revenge.

The canoe had not yet touched land when the girl leaped out as lightly as a fawn, not pausing to pick up her bow and quiver lying in the boat with her brother's. Turning around, she grasped the front of the craft with both hands, as if to draw it onto the bank.

Nantaquas rose to his feet, bending to pick up the bows and arrows. While he was doing so, the girl gave a lightning-fast sideways jerk to the boat, snapping it forward fully two feet. Thrown suddenly off balance, Nantaquas went backward over the side of the canoe and, as his heels kicked in the air, he dropped out of sight under the water.

Pocahontas screamed with delight. She had punished her brother as she planned. But her brother soon recovered and gave chase. She ran as fast as she could to get away, but ten to fifteen yards ahead stood an Indian, six feet tall, motionlessly surveying the couple with an inquiring expression. His long locks were sprinkled with gray, and his face was stern and lined with the passage of many stormy years. He was dressed like the younger warrior except that his face was unstained. In the belt around his waist were thrust a long knife and the handle of a tomahawk, but he carried no bow or quiver.

Hardly had the girl caught sight of him, when she ran forward and, throwing both arms around him, called out in panic: "Father, save me from Nantaquas! He wants to kill me!"

The father gazed at the young man and demanded: "What is the meaning of this?"

This was the famous chieftain, Powhatan. He ruled over numerous tribes, nearly all of whom he had conquered and brought under his sway. From Virginia to the far south he had no equal. Pocahontas, pretty and bright, was his favorite child and he permitted many liberties from her. Nantaquas was also a favorite, though Powhatan had other worthy sons.

"Let my child go home. Powhatan has something he would say to Nantaquas."

Pocahontas darted from sight and the chieftain continued: "The white men have come across the Deep Water to the hunting grounds of Powhatan and his people."

"Yes," the youth responded, "we met them on the river in their big canoes. They spoke words we did not understand, nor could they understand us. They have come to make their homes among us."

So Powhatan, from this and the signal fires he had read, knew of the coming of the Europeans while they were sailing up the James, several days before he saw any of them. Powhatan was deeply disturbed by the arrival of the English.

"They will come to land and build their wigwams. They will till the ground and hunt the game in the woods. By and by others will come and make their homes beside them; and they will keep on coming, until they are like the leaves on the trees. We have heard from the Indians of the south that they bring strange weapons that shoot fire and slay men who are beyond the reach of our arrows. They will kill our people or drive us into the sea, until none are left."

"The words of Powhatan are wise," said Nantaquas respectfully. "I am afraid of them and would not trust Pocahontas in their power."

"My son did right. She is but a child; she must stay away from them."

"And what shall be done with the white men?" asked Nantaquas. "Shall they be left alone when they go ashore, that their numbers may increase?—though I do not think they had any women with them."

"When the serpent is small, a child may crush it under the heel of her moccasin, but, if left to grow, it will soon sting her to death."

The meaning of these words was clear. Powhatan intended to destroy the colony before the white men could send for other friends to sail across the sea. Few though they were, this work would be hard and dangerous, when so little was known of their weapons; but no doubt, the thousands of warriors that Powhatan could summon to the task would do it well.

Powhatan, having made known his resolve, ordered his son to lead the way to where the canoe had been left. When they reached it, he stepped in and took his place at the bow.

By this time the afternoon was drawing to a close. The chieftain sat silent and erect, with no appearance of curiosity—but, nevertheless, with keen eyes. Passing back around the sweeping bend, the larger vessel and smaller ones came into view, lying at anchor close to the shore. It almost looked as though the white men were merely resting, waiting until the next day before going further upriver, except that smaller boats could be seen passing to and fro between the ships and the land.

Although it seemed little was to be feared from these unwelcome visitors at present, the life of Powhatan was too precious to permit any unnecessary risk to be run. He ordered his son to go a little nearer, holding himself ready to make instant flight when told to do so. Edging up, they were able to see three or four tents on a small peninsula jutting out from the northern shore. The white men had landed.

Nantaquas would have liked to visit the newcomers, now that his sister was not with him, but Powhatan would not allow it, and, at his command, the youth turned the head of the canoe upstream, before it had attracted notice, and quickly paddled away. As before, the chieftain did not speak, even after the boat had been run to land and drawn up on the beach. He stepped out, and with the majesty that was rarely absent, strode through the wilderness to his lodge, with his son walking silently in the rear. Once there, he held a long council with his chiefs and warriors. Plans for the destruction of the colony were drawn up; but before he slept that night, Pocahontas made him tell her all that had been agreed upon—and she did not rest until he had given his promise to postpone the dreadful work. He would not pledge himself to do more than postpone his designs, but this delay was of the greatest importance to the welfare of the little colony.

Chapter 3
Problems in the Colony

THE LOW PENINSULA that the newcomers had landed on was not an ideal site for a settlement—it was half-covered with water at high tide. But it looked so pleasant to the men who had been tossed about on the ocean for so many months that it was chosen as their new home. Anchor was dropped and boats began taking the men and their belongings to shore, and there, on May 13, 1607, they founded Jamestown. Like the James River, the settlement was called after King James, in whose name these colonists had come to conquer the "New" World.

As the English went ashore they pitched their tents, but the season was so mild that they found it more agreeable to make homes for the time being under the green leaves of the trees while building their cabins. These were built on the neck of the peninsula, and before long the place had taken on the look of a community. As soon as the hurry of work was over, a church building was put up. It was of modest size, sixty feet long and twenty-four feet wide.

It would seem that the best of beginnings had been made—but there was a flaw in the characters of the men. Very few had any fitness for pioneer work. Even those men whom the King had chosen as the colony's leaders were greedy and lazy, unwilling to do the work necessary to make the colony a success. Some of the other men thought themselves too good to perform any manual labor; back in England, they were "gentlemen," unused to physical work like clearing fields and planting crops.

Rumors of gold in the New World had drawn them across the ocean. They thought it

would only take a short time to load their
ships with the yellow metal, return to England
and live in luxury the rest of their days. Most
of those who did work for a living back in
England were jewelers and gold-refiners. John
Smith saw all this with anger and disgust.
However, he could do nothing about it now.
On the voyage across the Atlantic, there had
been a misunderstanding between him and
some of the other leaders. They accused him
of trying to gain control of the colony. While it
was true that Smith could be boastful and
overbearing at times, he was unselfish and
always thought of the interests of those who
were crossing the ocean with him to the New
World. As yet Smith had not had an opportunity to defend himself at a trial, and he could
not assume any sort of leadership role in
Jamestown, even though he was the ablest of
the men.

Shut out from the Council, he did not sulk,
though he felt the injustice. "By and by they
will ask for me," he thought.

He impressed upon his friends the need to
keep on good terms with the Indians. The season was far advanced, but the crops were
planted with the certainty that they would
ripen fast in that favorable climate and soil.
But the food brought over from England

would not last more than two or three months, and until the crops could be harvested, it would be necessary to obtain supplies from the Native Americans. If the Indians refused to trade with them, the Englishmen would suffer greatly.

Distrustful of Powhatan's attitude toward them, Captain Smith and a party of men took the first chance to sail up the river and pay a formal visit to the emperor of the country. The name of Powhatan's capital was also Powhatan, the chieftain being named after the town. This capital stood on a small hill, and numbered twelve houses, in front of which were three small islands in the river. The "palace" was a large structure of bark and skins, with a sort of bedstead on one side, on which Powhatan sat with his majestic mien, his robe of raccoon skins, and the feathers in his grizzled hair, a king upon his throne.

When Smith and two of his companions were brought into the presence of this emperor, the scene was striking. Along each wall of the dwelling stood two rows of young women at the rear and two rows of men in front of them. The faces of all the women were stained with the red juice of the *puccoon* and a number wore chains of white beads around their necks. Smith doffed his hat, made a sweeping bow and addressed Powhatan with as much outward respect as if the Indian chief had been the King of England.

One proof of John Smith's ability was that during his brief stay in Virginia he had been able to pick up enough knowledge of the Powhatan language to make himself fairly well understood with the help of gestures. There had been Indian visitors from the first at Jamestown, too. All were treated so well that several spent much of their time at the settlement, studying the white men and their ways. Smith took this opportunity to learn from these Indians, and was thus able to tell Powhatan that he and the other Englishmen had come across the Great Water with feelings only of love for him and his people. They had no wish to take away their hunting grounds, nor to kill their game, nor to do them harm in any way. He hinted that the whites might prove to be of great help to Powhatan, for they brought strange and deadly weapons with them, which they would be glad to use in helping him to conquer other Indian tribes.

Captain Smith was a man of rare tact, but he blundered when he made this offer to the old emperor. It implied that Powhatan was not able to conquer the rebellious tribes on his own. Powhatan was so self-confident that any hint that he might need help in carrying out his own will was an insult to him. Smith was quick to recognize his mistake, and did what he could to correct it, but he did not succeed. Powhatan was irritated and it was clear that he felt no good will toward those who dared to make their homes in his country. He pretended not to understand the broken sentences of his visitor until one of his warriors helped to interpret them. Unable to convince Powhatan of the settlers' peaceful intentions, Smith and his friends withdrew and set sail down the river for Jamestown.

During the interview both Smith and his companions asked about the youth and the girl who had met them when they first sailed up the James. But neither Nantaquas nor Pocahontas was present, a fact that proved they were absent from the town—no other reason would have kept them from the palace on so interesting an occasion.

Chapter 4

Signals and Shots

WITH THE COMING of the hot, sultry southern summer all prudence seemed to leave the settlers. They drank the unwholesome water, and the mosquitos that bred in the swamps carried malaria. Many of the colonists contracted the disease, and those who remained healthy thought it too uncomfortable to work when the sun was overhead. Later, as night drew near, the day was too far gone to labor. They could not be roused early enough in the day to do anything worthwhile. The president of the colony, Edward Wingfield, set the example of indolence—and instead of eating moderately, acted as if there could never be an end to the nearly exhausted food supply.

While the future looked so dark, Smith was more disturbed by the present. He saw in the resentful manner of Powhatan something more than displeasure with the white men's presence. Holding as much power as he did, the chief was not likely to remain quiet for long. He surely knew of the growing weakness of the colonists—short of food, plagued by sickness and the certainty that they would soon be at the mercy of the Indians.

Smith wondered why an attack had not been made on the English long before. With the many warriors that Powhatan could summon, they would have been able to crush the little band of Europeans, despite their fire-arms. Smith had no idea that the postponement of such an assault was due to Pocahontas—nor did he learn the truth until years afterward.

As his boat was making the slow moonlit journey back to Jamestown from Powhatan's village, a peculiar flickering toward the northern shore caught Smith's eye—it was an Indian canoe, in which he made out one person handling the paddle, with a companion sitting quietly in the stern. The Captain recalled the sight that had greeted the ships when first coming up the James. There was the small craft, driven in the same manner, with the same number of persons. Smith watched it closely and was soon certain that the two persons were Nantaquas and Pocahontas. He had learned their identity from the friendly Indians who came to Jamestown: the plume worn by the girl was a badge of royalty.

The canoe was passing the bow of the ship a hundred yards distant, making no attempt to

come nearer. Wanting to talk, Smith called out:
"Nantaquas! Will you not come aboard?"

The youth seemed to exchange words with his sister, after which he headed his craft in the direction of the larger one. A few minutes would have brought him alongside, but he was brought up short by a startling interruption. Through the stillness a low, booming sound rolled upstream and echoed along the shore.

It was the sound of the small cannon on the *Susan Constant*, many miles downstream, and it meant danger to Jamestown. The single blast alarmed Captain Smith and his friends, for to them it could only have one meaning. It had been fired because of an attack by Indians on the settlement. The detonation carried the same message to Powhatan's son and daughter, who had been drawing near the large boat in response to Smith's invitation. Nantaquas plied his paddle with renewed vigor, but instantly veered away. Indeed, the youth expected a volley from the boat, but nothing of the kind occurred to Smith, who did not interfere while the canoe and its occupants rapidly passed from sight.

Smith hurried to the stern, where the others had gathered around the steersman. "The settlement has been attacked," he said. "Listen!"

Naturally, the certainty that there was trouble at Jamestown increased Smith's and his friends' impatience to reach the place as soon as they could. But the fates were against them for the time. The wind had stopped and the rising tide began to carry them back to Powhatan's capital. The anchor dropped and the craft lay at rest, waiting for the tide to turn or the wind to rise. Two men were placed on guard and the others got what sleep they could.

The calm lasted through the night and when daylight came the surface of the James was as smooth as glass. The tide had turned, but moved so slowly that Captain Smith told his skipper to let the anchor remain dropped for a few hours. They ate sparingly of the coarse bread they had brought and the fowl that Smith had shot on the upward voyage.

Smith's next words caused astonishment. He intended to go to the southern shore with two of the men to discover the meaning of the signal fire he had seen the night before. He hoped to learn something of the trouble at Jamestown, but he also wanted to find a way to obtain grain, which his countrymen needed. He knew that a small Indian village was not far inland. There was reason to hope that through barter or, as a last resort, a display of force, the villagers could be persuaded to part with a good supply of food.

A number of trinkets, beads, ribbons and knives were bundled up and put in the boat, and the three men took their places. With the Captain at the stern, the two others began rowing. Smith studied the shore, hoping some of the warriors would show themselves, though none did.

Chapter 5

Captain Smith Protects Pocahontas

WHEN THE BOAT touched land, the three stepped out and awaited Smith's orders. Each man had a knife, a cumbersome, heavy flintlock musket and ammunition. Feeling he could do better alone, Captain Smith told his friends to follow the course of the stream—never wandering so far into the woods that they could not easily make their way back to the water. If they met any Indians or made any important discoveries, they were to call at the top of their voices and he would run over and take charge of things. Smith then took a different path.

The only sign of the recent presence of others was the heap of ashes left by the signal fire, which had been kindled within a few feet of the stream. The two men, Jack Bertram and Dan Wood, moved upstream—in the direction of Powhatan's village. There was no reason to think they would find anything interesting by keeping to the river, so they went inland for some distance and then took a course parallel with the river.

The timber was dense and the undergrowth so matted it was hard to force a passage. Wood walked in front, making the work easier for Bertram, who kept close behind. When they had pushed their way a short distance, Wood stopped.

"What good can come of this? No one has been this way—so we can't catch up with anybody."

"They might be coming from the other way," said his companion, less discouraged because he had been doing less work.

"Little chance of that. I don't understand what Captain Smith hopes to learn or do by this groping through the woods. If we knew the way to the Indian village we could go there and if they would not give us food, take it from them! Ah! I wasn't looking for this!"

Turning to resume their passage through the forest, Wood had caught sight of a well-marked trail leading over the course they were following.

"It has been made by animals coming to the river to drink," said Bertram. "It can be of no help to us, though it may also be used by people."

Wood walked for a few paces, scanning the path, which soon turned to the left, leading farther inland. Suddenly he stood still. Glancing up, Bertram saw the reason for it, and was as much astonished as his companion.

Standing in the trail, staring at the two men, was the very girl they had seen when the ships were sailing up the James weeks before on their way to found the colony. She had the same rich robe around her shoulders and the same white plume curling over her long black hair. She carried her long bow in one hand, the top of a quiver of arrows peeping from behind her left shoulder.

She caught sight of the white men before they saw her. She must have been coming over the path when she observed the figures and stopped in amazement.

"It is Pocahontas," whispered Bertram. "We

did not see her yesterday at the old chief's lodge. I wonder what she can be doing here alone?"

"Her friends can't be far off. But I say, Jack, this is a godsend."

"What do you mean?"

"You'll see."

The girl did not hesitate once she realized that she had been observed by the strangers. She knew where these men had come from and she came smilingly forward. She had noticed the custom of the Englishmen of clasping their hands when they met. Without pausing, she reached out her hand to Wood, who was in front, and said to him in broken words:

"How do? How do? Me friend—you friend."

Wood took her hand, warmly pressed it, and then gave way to Bertram, who did the same. Pocahontas tried to say something more, but she knew so little English that neither caught her meaning. She saw that too many of her words were spoken in her own tongue, so, laughing, she gave up the effort and stood looking inquiringly into the faces before her.

"Jack," said Wood in a low voice, "the Indians have attacked Jamestown. We don't know how many of our people they have killed. We need food. Let's take this daughter of the old chief and hold her hostage. We'll give him the choice of letting us have all the corn we want—or of having his pet daughter put to death."

"I hardly know what to say to that. It might not work."

"It has to. Powhatan loves her so much that he will do anything to keep her from coming to harm."

Wood did not wait to argue further, but, taking a quick step toward the smiling girl, grasped her upper arm. In answer to her questioning look he said:

"Go with us. We take you to Jamestown. Won't hurt."

The smiles gave way to an expression of alarm. She held back.

"No, no, no! Me no go! Powhatan feel bad—much bad!"

"You must go!" said Wood, tightening his grip. "We not hurt you any."

Bertram stood silent—he didn't like the scheme that had been suddenly sprung upon him, but he thought it might turn out well, so he didn't interfere.

And then Pocahontas began crying and striving to wrench her arm free. Had not Wood used all his strength, she would have gotten away. Impatient over her resistance, he

tried to scare her into submission. Scowling
at her, he said, in a brutal tone:

"Stop! Come with me or I will kill you!"

This was an idle threat. He thought nothing
of the kind. But he probably would have
struck her, for he was a quick-tempered man.
Pocahontas struggled harder than ever, her
moccasins sliding over the slippery leaves,
tears streaming down her cheeks. She begged
and prayed in her own language, not knowing
the English words.

Captain Smith had only gone a little way
down the stream when he decided that he had
taken the wrong course. He turned around
and followed after his companions, coming
upon them in the midst of the struggle
between Wood and Powhatan's young daughter. He paused only an instant, when he
angrily cried out:

"What is the meaning of this?"

Wood merely glanced around at his leader
and kept on dragging the captive along the
trail. It was Bertram who hastily said:

"She is the daughter of Powhatan. We are
going to take her to Jamestown as a hostage
and make the chieftain give us food——"

Without waiting for anything further, the
Captain sprang forward, shouting wrathfully:

"Let her go! Release her!"

Before the amazed fellow could comply, he was grasped by the back of the collar. Captain Smith shifted his gun to his right hand, so as to leave the other free. The fingers were like those of a giant, and the frightened English-man let go of his sobbing prisoner. As he did so the Captain gave a kick with his right foot that lifted Wood clear of the ground, sending him tumbling on his face, his peaked hat fall-ing off and his gun flying several yards away.

"I would do right to kill you!" cried Smith, his face aflame as he glared down on the fel-low, who began climbing to his feet. "There is not one so good a friend of the English among all the Indians as this little girl."

As he spoke he pointed toward the spot where Pocahontas had stood only a minute before, but she was not there. She had instantly taken advantage of her release and had fled beyond sight.

Captain Smith's burst of anger was caused, in the first place, by the unpardonable vio-lence shown to the young and gentle Poca-hontas. In the sweetness of her nature she had shown perfect trust in the white men and all knew she had only friendship for the peo-ple who had made their homes in the country of her father, the great Powhatan. What a rude awakening for her! What harm would it bring

The Captain gave a kick with his right foot that lifted
Wood clear of the ground, sending him tumbling on
his face.

to those who so badly needed the good will of the powerful tribes around them?

A second cause of the Captain's wrath was the fact that the outrage, apart from its wickedness, was the worst thing possible. If Wood had succeeded in taking Pocahontas hostage, Powhatan would not have been frightened into helping the Englishmen; the act would have added to his ill will.

Not only that, but the immediate results were sure to be disastrous. It was not to be supposed that Pocahontas was alone so far from her home. She certainly had friends near at hand—she was already fleeing with her story—she would reach them soon and they would hasten to punish her enemies.

These thoughts flashed through the mind of Captain Smith, while the victim of his anger was slowly climbing to his feet. He took a step toward Wood, meaning to strike him to the earth again, but the man shrank away, with no word of protest. The Captain checked himself and said:

"We must hasten to the boat before we are cut off. Come!"

The fellow picked up his hat and gun, and Captain Smith led the way at a rapid pace over the trail and through the underbrush, till they reached the edge of the stream, along which they hurried to the spot where the craft had been drawn up. Smith pushed it free and stepped inside. He took his place at the bow, facing the shore they were leaving, as did the two who sat down and hastily caught up the oars.

Neither of the men had spoken a word since Smith's rescue of Pocahontas, and they bent to their oars with the utmost energy. They knew they had done wrong, and nothing was left but to obey the command of their leader, which they did with the proper good will.

The three had reached a point fifty yards from land when a young Indian warrior dashed through the undergrowth into the open space on the beach. He was Nantaquas—at his side was Pocahontas. He held his bow and had drawn an arrow from his quiver. The girl pointed excitedly to Wood, who was nearer to them than the other two men.

"Look out!" warned the Captain. "He means to shoot you!"

The endangered fellow was so flustered that he broke the regular strokes of the oars, and Bertram strove hard to keep the boat on its course. Wood kept his eyes on the young warrior, who rigidly straightened his left arm, with the hand gripping the middle of the bow, while he drew the feathered arrow to its head and aimed at the alarmed man.

Captain Smith watched Nantaquas, not allowing any movement to escape him. Suddenly he called, *"Down!"*

Wood instantly flung himself forward on his face, so that he was hidden by the low side of the boat. Bertram dodged to one side. The Captain did not move. He knew *he* was in no danger.

At the same time that the oarsmen went down Nantaquas launched his arrow, which came with such swiftness that the eye could hardly follow. The missile streaked over the spot where Wood had just been sitting, fired with such accuracy that, but for his quickness, the arrow would have been buried in his chest.

So great was the power with which the missile was fired that it seemed to dart horizontally outward for nearly a hundred feet beyond the boat before it dipped enough for the point to drop into the water.

In the few seconds that had passed since Nantaquas fired, Wood partly regained his coolness. He raised his head, but instead of

drawing on his oars, he reached for the musket at his feet. His companion kept toiling
with all his strength.

"Drop that!" thundered Captain Smith. "It
would serve you right if you were killed! Use
your oars!"

At any moment the Captain could have shot
Nantaquas, who stood out in clear view,—as
could either of his companions—but the
leader would not allow it. He sympathized
with the Indian, and though he did not care to
have Wood slain, he would not permit any
harm to be done to Nantaquas.

The youth had fitted another arrow to his
bow, and Captain Smith noted every movement. Nantaquas saw that if he fired again,
and the man serving as his target dodged, the
arrow was likely to hit Captain Smith, unless
he was equally quick in eluding it. The distance was increasing and every second added
to the difficulty of the shot. He knew which
man had befriended Pocahontas, and eager as
he was to slay the criminal, he would have to
forgo that pleasure in order to spare the
friend.

Holding the bow poised for a few seconds,
he slowly lowered it, still keeping the notch
of the arrow pressed against the string, as
if expecting a new chance to present itself.

Holding the bow poised for a few seconds, he slowly
lowered it, still keeping the notch of the arrow
pressed against the string.

If the boat would turn sideways toward him, as at first, he might still bring down his man—but the boat moved rapidly and soon passed beyond bowshot.

Nantaquas remained standing in full view on the shore, his sister beside him, both watching the receding craft until it came alongside the large one. The three men stepped aboard, leaving the small boat to be towed at the stern. Then brother and sister turned about and passed from sight into the forest.

A brisk breeze was blowing, and Captain Smith and his companions had hardly rejoined their friends when the anchor was hoisted, and they were carried at a good speed toward Jamestown, which they reached early that afternoon. There they learned that the settlement had just passed through a trying experience.

Chapter 6
Smith Helps the Settlers

ALTHOUGH THE Englishmen had arrived at the site of Jamestown rather late in the season for planting, and although many of them were too lazy to work, others did what they could to make up for lost time. In the rich soil, which had been cleared of trees, corn that had been obtained from the Indians was planted, and quickly showed a vigor of growth that promised the best results.

On the day that Captain Smith sailed up the James to make his call of state upon Powhatan, more than twenty men were engaged in planting and cultivating the corn already put in the ground. Without any warning, from the woods nearby came confusing showers of arrows. Only occasional glimpses of the shouting Indians could be seen as they flitted from tree to tree, using the trunks as shields. The panic-stricken English dropped their tools and ran behind the stockades, which had been finished only a short time before. Those who glanced behind saw one man lying on his face, dead, pierced by so many arrows that he looked like a porcupine. Nearly all the others had been hit, some of them two or three times—when they ran through the open gate the arrows were still sticking in their bodies and clothing. Seventeen men had been wounded, most of them only slightly, though three or four looked as if they might die of their wounds. All, however, recovered.

Instead of leaving, the Indians kept their places in the woods, continually launching their arrows at the settlers. While these were harmless when directed against the stockades, some of the warriors curved them so that they dropped inside the defenses. It required careful watching on the part of the settlers to keep from being badly hurt—a sharp-pointed missile coming straight down from a height of more than a hundred feet could be fatal. The Englishmen could protect themselves, but were unable to drive off their attackers while they were so well shielded among the trees.

This is how things stood when the *Susan Constant* came on the scene. Dropping a little way downstream, so as to get clear range of the woods, she discharged two of her cannon that were loaded to the muzzle with slugs. It is not likely that any of the warriors were hurt, but when they saw large limbs splintered and falling about their heads, and heard the rattle among the leaves and twigs overhead and all about them, they were terrified and scurried off in panic.

Not another foe was seen during the day, though there could be no doubt that many pairs of eyes were peeping from the vegetation—wondering what kind of weapon could tear whole branches from trees. Some time after dark, the settlers heard sounds in the woods that showed that their enemies had returned. The *Susan Constant*, which had held her place after driving off the Indians earlier in the day, now fired another shot, and this ended all trouble of that sort for some time to follow. It was the booming of this cannon that had traveled up the James to the boat where Captain Smith sat meditatively smoking.

The first attack on Jamestown brought good results. It was clear to all that the settlement must have an industrious leader and that he must be a military man. Wingfield, lazy and greedy as he was, had no qualifications whatever for the office. He had to be replaced or the colony would be ruined. Smith was determined to remove Wingfield from office and demanded his own right to a trial. Smith knew that once he could clear himself of the charges made on the voyage from England, he could assume his rightful place on the Council and help the other colonists.

Wingfield refused, and when Smith insisted, the president replied that he would send Smith back to England to be tried by the authorities.

"You will not!" said the angry Captain. "The charter provides for the trial of all such charges in Virginia; it is my right, and I will not be denied it."

So, against his will, Wingfield gave Smith his trial, which was the first trial by jury in America; and never did an accused man gain a greater triumph. Every charge brought against him was shown to be false; the witnesses broke down and those who had sworn that Smith had plotted against the colony were proven to have sworn falsely. Smith was not only declared innocent of the charges, but his chief persecutor, a member of the Council, was ordered to pay over to him a fine of 200 pounds. When this large sum of money was presented to Smith, he gave it to the colony for general use. Then all parties took Communion, declared themselves friends and Smith took his seat as a member of the Council.

He had no wish to be president, though he

knew the day was near when no one else would be able to save the colony. He had a freer hand in many matters while simply a Councillor—and wanted people to become tired of Wingfield before he would consider stepping into his shoes.

The miseries of that first summer in Jamestown were enormous. For a time it looked as if disease would claim the life of every man. They lay groaning in fever and agony—so that even the danger from the Indians was forgotten. If Powhatan had wanted to attack Jamestown with only twenty warriors he would have had no trouble in wiping out the colony. Even the sturdy Captain Smith took ill with fever, but he did not give up, and assisted in the task of burying the dead. Some of those who died were missed sadly, for they were good men, willing to work to save Jamestown.

There remained, however, the corrupt president Wingfield and the Council member whom Smith had defeated at his trial. These two were Smith's bitter enemies and they formed a plot that, if successful, would ruin not only Smith, but the entire colony as well.

By September, half the Jamestown settlers had passed away and most of the survivors were tottering with weakness and disease.

For weeks these wretches could not have raised a hand to ward off the Indians had they chosen to attack. But the Native Americans were moved to pity and they brought corn to the sufferers, though only enough to last a short time.

Captain Newport had sailed back to England several months before for food and supplies, but he was not expected back for a long time. He left one of the smaller boats for the colonists' use, and Wingfield and his friend plotted to steal it and sail back to England, leaving the other settlers stranded. Their plot failed, however, and the others were so indignant that they removed them from the Council, and chose John Ratcliffe as president. He was not much better than Wingfield, though, and the settlers soon demanded that Smith take charge.

The Captain quickly proved his worth. He made people understand that every well man must either work or starve. He would have no idlers, and set the example by working as hard as the best of them. On his return from an expedition down the river, where he forced a hostile tribe to trade corn with him, he arrived just as Wingfield and his friend made another attempt to seize the colony's boat. Just as the two scoundrels were about to set sail, Smith opened fire on them with a cannon and would have sunk the craft had they not surrendered. Their action was so wicked that they were tried by jury. The life of Wingfield was spared, though he was stripped of all authority. His companion was condemned to death and shot.

Chapter 7
Smith Goes Exploring

WITH THE COMING of the cool weather a great improvement took place in the health of the colonists. Disease subsided and fever disappeared. Those who had been ill rapidly regained their well-being. The river abounded with fish and fowl, and the ripening corn was made into bread. The future looked bright for the first time—even though many had died. Other immigrants were sure to arrive soon—perhaps they were on the way even then.

When things improved, the colonists Smith had saved complained because he had not done more. He gave up the presidency, as the best means of teaching the people to value him.

The Council also reprimanded Captain Smith because he had not begun to search for the South Sea—one of the reasons the King of England had sponsored the settlement. The councillors believed that once the South Sea was found, trade routes could be established that would make them rich men. Smith replied to their criticism by declaring that he would set out at once. It would be a great relief to get away from the quarreling people, and the expedition would fulfill his desire for adventure.

On a clear, cold day early in December, Smith started on his voyage in a barge propelled by a crew of six Englishmen and two friendly Indians. He trailed a smaller boat behind the barge to ascend further when the river narrowed. It could also be used for hunting game that would be scared away by the sight of the larger boat.

The barge was provided with a sail, which would be helpful at least part of the time. It also had a small half-cabin at the stern in which the off-duty shift could sleep. There were plenty of blankets, though fire was not used as a means of warmth. There were three oarlocks on each side, to be used when the wind was not strong enough. A scant supply of cornbread and venison was brought, but the party planned to rely on the fish they would catch from the stream and the fowl and game they would shoot along the shore or in the woods.

When the barge left Jamestown, not a flake of snow was to be seen anywhere, though winter had begun—and the climate in Virginia is sometimes severe. A strong breeze was blowing from the east, so the craft moved easily without the use of oars. Captain Smith planned to travel up the Chickahominy River, which empties into the James from a source far to the west. Most of this river flowed through swampy areas choked by fallen trees, which made navigation difficult. Captain Smith had sailed a few miles above the mouth of the Chickahominy some weeks before, but this new region was unknown to him. But this made the journey more pleasant for Smith, for he could never resist the prospect of adventure.

It was still early in the day when the barge entered the broad mouth of the Chickahominy. Captain Smith sat at the stern, just behind the little cabin, his hand resting on the tiller. Seated thus, the explorer was in a good position to study the country as they moved between the banks. Everyone was alert, for they were entering the hunting grounds of the Chickahominy Indians.

About the middle of the afternoon the breeze fell and the flapping sail told the navigator that they must use the oars. The Indians sat near the bow, silent and watchful; they were scanning the shores, alert for any sign of danger.

Suddenly one of the Indians uttered a hissing sound that all heard, faint though it was. The men stopped rowing and Captain Smith looked inquiringly at the Indians. One pointed ahead to the right bank. The river at this point was more than two hundred yards wide, the trees growing close to the shore and many in the water itself.

In answer to Smith's inquiry the Indian said, in his own tongue, that an Indian warrior was near them on the shore. There might be more, but there was at least one. After a moment, the Captain ordered the oarsmen to continue rowing. As they did he steered the boat a little to the left, but kept his attention riveted to the spot where possible danger lurked.

The man was right, for all who were on the watch saw two warriors, partly hidden by the trees and undergrowth, crouching and staring at the barge. One of them seemed to be fixing an arrow to the string of his bow. He suddenly aimed and let fly his arrow, which passed ten feet over the heads of the crew and dropped into the water beyond.

Captain Smith quickly reached down and took up his musket. He aimed at the daring warrior and pulled the trigger. The warrior was struck, throwing him into a panic. With a yell he whirled on his feet and dashed into the wood with his equally startled companion at his heels.

Smith had done a prudent thing, for, had he not returned fire, his foes would have thought the white men were afraid and would have continued their attack. Nothing further of that nature was to be feared from the two warriors or any of their friends.

The barge continued its way up the Chicka-hominy until night began closing in. By that time they had reached the edge of the White Oak Swamp, where lagoons and wide-spreading ponds or lakes were choked with trees and shal-low in places. Thinking it would be safer to stay aboard the barge than to camp on shore, Smith ordered the men to drop anchor in the middle of one of these small lakes.

After night had fully come, the anchor was gently lifted and the position of the craft was shifted a fair distance downstream. Any war-

He suddenly aimed and let fly his arrow.

riors in the area would seek it where it was last seen in the gathering gloom, and failing to find it, would look elsewhere.

Two men were assigned guard duty, one at the bow, the other at the stern, near the small cabin. As Captain Smith gave them this duty he warned them to be on the alert every minute. Their orders were to fire on anything suspicious, for, in so doing, they would teach their enemies an important lesson. At midnight, they were to call two of the others and change places with them.

"Gunpowder is valuable," added the Captain. "Don't waste it!"

The men had held their guard for nearly two hours without hearing or seeing anything suspicious. Deep, impenetrable darkness shut in the boat. There was no danger of the men falling asleep at their post. They might have done so had they tried to watch until daybreak—as it was, they continued vigilantly, as if pacing in front of a campfire.

Suddenly, near the end of the watch, the man at the bow heard a sound that he knew meant danger. It was so faint that he did not know what it was or where it was coming from. He pushed the blanket that he had wrapped about him from his ears and listened. Thinking that the noise had been on his

right, he leaned forward in an effort to pene-
trate the gloom and reached for his musket.

Five to ten minutes of silence followed,
when he heard the noise again—still faint, but
clear enough to reveal its nature and direction. It was the sound of a paddle—and he
had been right about the direction it came
from. Without a doubt, a party of Indians in a
canoe were quietly heading for the barge.

The man did not signal to his companion,
but leaned farther over the gunwale and
peered into the darkness. He lifted his gun so
that it lay across his knee, and smothering the
click made by the lock, he drew back the
hammer.

Straining his eyes, he made out something
shadowy resting on the water. It was moving
very slowly, neither approaching the barge
nor retreating from it, but seemingly circling
it. It was a canoe, and instead of completing
its circle, it paused just in front of the barge's
bow.

The lookout thought that it would not stay
motionless for long, but pass on, probably
coming closer to the barge—but minutes
passed without any change in its position.
Several times while he was watching he was
sure that there really was nothing in sight,
but, upon shifting his gaze for a moment and

bringing it back, his doubt disappeared. The canoe was there, though he could not make out how many people were in it.

Uncertain as to what to do, the guard called cautiously to his companion, who made his way stealthily to his side.

"Have you seen anything strange?" he whispered.

"Nothing whatever. How about you?"

"A few yards in front of us a canoe is holding still; I can barely see it, and I don't know whether or not to fire. What do you think?"

With a hand on his friend's shoulder, the other guard leaned far over the rail and looked into the gloom.

"It's there—and it is full of warriors."

"Then I'll do as Captain Smith ordered."

"And I'll wait to see what happens before I fire."

The first guard raised his gunstock to his shoulder, dropping his blanket to leave his arms free. He sighted carefully, but hesitated because he couldn't fix his vision on the target. It seemed to melt away in the darkness.

"I can't see it," he muttered. "You fire."

"There's no point—it's gone."

During the brief moments taken to aim, the canoe had glided off in the dark, and the sharpest observer would not have been able to locate it. The guards moved back to their posts and the two kept watch until well after midnight. Then they woke two of their friends and told them what they had seen. The following watch discovered nothing to cause alarm, nor was the canoe seen or heard from again. The warriors, after studying the large boat, probably had agreed that it was too dangerous for them to attack, and went away.

The two following days were disheartening. The sail only helped propel the barge upriver for a short time, and there were hours when the oars were useless because of the many obstacles. Three times the crew had to saw their way through the branches and more than once, after long and strenuous effort, they could not move forward at all. Fortunately they were not attacked. On the second day a lone warrior was seen jumping from log to log across one of the many streams. He whisked out of sight the moment his moccasins hit dry land.

Finally, the large boat was of no further use in going upstream. The small one would now have to be used. It had served well when they had to saw their way through the choked waters. Smith could have turned back and explored other branches of the James, but he had given his word to the Council. He would go up the Chickahominy as far as he could.

Chapter 8
Attack on Smith's Men

THE DAY WAS almost over, so Smith decided to wait until the next morning to continue the journey. Although they had only seen one warrior after the exchange of shots several days before, Smith was not convinced that he and his crew were safe from attack by the Indians whose hunting grounds they were now on. He sent his Indian scouts ashore to scour the woods for signs of warriors or hunting parties, and urged the guards to remain watchful through the night.

Smith was watchful, too. As he waited for the scouts' return, many disturbing questions crossed his mind. What if, wondered Smith, the Indians seen earlier had friends nearby and he had told them of the white men's approach? Would they try to kill the white men? Smith did not know.

The scouts did not come back until late at night. They reported that they had not seen any sign of their own people in the vicinity. The men keeping watch on the boat had not noticed anything suspicious either. It seemed that they were not in danger, and yet Smith knew that almost anything could happen. Perhaps the Indians knew the white men were looking for them, and so kept out of sight. Or maybe the Indian scouts had reached an agreement with the warriors, and knew how many there were but weren't telling Smith. All of these unanswered questions made the night seem very long.

The next morning, the barge was rowed to the middle of a wide stretch of water with the woods far off in every direction; the anchor was dropped into the soft bottom. Smith planned to proceed up the river in the smaller boat and he wanted to take the two scouts and two of the other men with him.

It would be much easier to go up the Chickahominy in the smaller boat and Smith thought he could continue the ascent of the river for several days. He meant to press on as far he could go in the boat. Whether he should continue on foot would depend on circumstances.

"No matter what happens after I am gone,"

he told the four who stayed on the barge, "not one of you is to go ashore. That might be what the Indians are waiting for you to do. Stay here until I get back."

"But, suppose, Captain," said one with a grin, "you do not come back?"

"Wait for three days. If you see nothing of me then, turn the boat downstream and make all haste to Jamestown."

"And what shall we say when we get there?"

"Say what you please," replied the Captain impatiently. "I have no doubt you will sprinkle plenty of falsehood in your words."

So five men entered the boat, which had two pairs of oars but no sail. The white men did the rowing, while the Indians stoically looked on.

Captain Smith had not been gone half an hour when those left behind in the barge started grumbling.

"It is unbearable to stay here for two or three days," said one man seated at the bow, looking glum. "How shall we spend the weary hours?"

"We could fish," said another, grinning.

"That would do for a little while, but the fish do not bite graciously in this wintry weather, and we'll grow tired."

"The scouts told us no Indians were near; that should satisfy us. Let's go ashore, where we can find game and stretch our limbs."

The proposal was in violation of their leader's orders, but it appealed to all four men. Two rose to their feet and began plying their poles. The water was five or six feet deep and the craft began sliding toward land. While the two toiled the others scanned the woods they were nearing. Each laid his musket across his knees.

The point they were heading for was a space favorable for stepping from the craft. All around stretched the forest, with its dense thickets and matted vines.

The side of the boat was so near the bank that it was a short jump for any of them. One man stood still with his pole, ready to jump, when one of his friends, who had gotten up, gun in hand, shouted out:

"Back—quick! The woods are full of Indians!"

The four white men on the boat did not lose their presence of mind. The two polesmen worked quickly, despite the arrows whizzing around them. The boat moved rapidly and the space between it and the shore widened with every moment. Their companions aimed their muskets at the crowding forms, and fired with such skill that each brought down a warrior. The other warriors darted back among the trees, hiding behind the trunks and continuing to launch their arrows at the men in the boat.

No one could have shown more bravery than the two men plying the poles. They paid no attention to the missiles flying around them, while their companions reloaded and discharged the guns as quickly as possible. When the craft reached the middle of the river little was to be feared from the Indians, for the distance was too great for them to aim well.

At this moment something strange happened. The clothes of all the defenders had been pierced by arrows—some in several places, and two had been wounded, though not severely. The man who had been the most exposed, standing out in full view while helping to pole the boat, was the only one of the four who was not so much as scratched. Another had been hit, but was smiling over his good fortune at surviving the attack, when he pitched forward on his face, pierced to the heart by one of the last arrows to be fired.

The body was tenderly laid in the stern, and then, while two men held their weapons ready, the third used the oars. There was no thought now of staying where they were until Captain Smith came back. They did not believe he would ever come back. So they kept on downstream as best they could. Fortunately for them the band of Indians did not follow along the banks—and with the help of the current, they made good progress. In due course they glided out of the mouth of the Chickahominy into the James and, reaching Jamestown, told their story. Among the settlers no one expected ever to see Captain John Smith and his companions again.

Chapter 9

Smith Is Captured

WHILE THE MEN on the barge were fighting for their lives, Smith and his party had traveled about a dozen miles before meeting their first barrier. Smith saw the little boat could go no further. He had strayed from the river itself and was following one of its branches. He did not like that, so, telling the oarsmen to turn to the left bank, all stepped out, and the boat was drawn up nearly out of the water.

"You are weary from rowing," he said to the oarsmen. "Wait here while I go a little farther in search of game."

"Can't we help you?" asked one, who added that they were not tired. Both would have been glad to take part in the hunt.

Captain Smith preferred that only the scouts go with him, so he told his friends to stay where they were. He meant to return before dark, when they could broil the game which he was sure of bagging, and they would spend the night in comfort by the campfire in the heart of the forest.

Despite what the men said, they were quite worn out from rowing. After Smith left, they kindled a big fire, wrapped their blankets around them and lay down with their feet to the fire. By and by they sank into deep, restful sleep. Sadly, neither of them ever awoke. At the end of an hour, while they lay dreaming, the same party of Indians that had attacked the barge found them and quickly ended their lives.

The leader of this band was called Opecan-canough, who was one of Powhatan's brothers and a very powerful warrior; if anything happened to Powhatan, Opecancanough was the man most likely to become Emperor.

Opecancanough never liked the English, and he frequently urged Powhatan and his fellow warriors to destroy them before their numbers became too great to overcome. He had much to do with the hostility his older brother often showed to the settlers.

Opecancanough knew that Captain John Smith was the leading man at Jamestown, and that it was more important to kill him than to get rid of twenty other Englishmen. When he learned of the Chickahominy expedition, he gathered more than a hundred of his warriors and secretly followed the boat for many miles, waiting for a chance to destroy the crew, but especially to slay Captain Smith. Opecancanough had pursued Smith and his men for many miles without the white men suspecting a thing.

When Captain Smith and his companions started up the branch of the Chickahominy in the smaller boat, the Indians were on the other side of the broad expanse of water and did not see them leave. And when the barge began working toward shore, Opecancanough believed that Smith and the entire crew were still on board. During the fight, however, the chief saw that five of the men, including the Captain, were gone. He noticed, also, that the small rowboat that had been towed at the stern was missing. Opecancanough then realized that Captain Smith must have gone upstream with four companions.

Though Opecancanough had made one slip, he didn't intend to make another. He and his warriors applied all of their tracking skills, searching for clues as to Smith's whereabouts. Studying carefully the different outlets of the expanse of water, Opecancanough noticed a slight disturbance caused by the passage of the small boat. Other signs became clearer as they pressed along the shore, leaving no doubt that they were on the right track. Eventually, they arrived at the camp where the two Englishmen lay asleep. After that fatal encounter, the Indians pushed on after Captain Smith.

It was not hard to trail the Captain and the two scouts, since Smith could not go through the forest without leaving the prints of his shoes, which were as easy to follow as if he had been walking over a dusty road. By this time, Smith had no thoughts of danger. Having come so far in the wilderness without trouble, he thought all threats had passed. Only one incident, after he had gone a little way, caused

misgiving. He kept the lead, the Indians following him in single file, as was their custom.
Smith tramped forward, sometimes turning to
avoid a dense growth of underbrush. He was
peering among the branches of the trees and
along the ground in front and on either side in
search of game, and was growing impatient.
Suddenly he saw a movement among the trees
to the left that he knew was caused by some
animal. Uttering a guarded "Shh!," he stopped
short and looked keenly at the point where he
had seen the movement.

The next moment he caught the outlines of
a noble buck walking among the trees, with
his side turned toward the hunter. The deer
had not noticed the hunter yet, though it was
sure to detect him soon. Afraid that the Indians might not see the animal, Smith turned his
head to whisper a warning.

As he did so he saw only one of his men.
The one who had been at the rear was gone.
This discovery caused such a shudder of dis-
trust that Smith forgot the buck moving a little way from him and asked: "Where is he?"

The second scout flashed his head about,
and seemed as astonished as the white man.
He answered in his own tongue: "He was
walking behind me; I do not know what has
become of him."

Both looked among the trees to the left and right and rear, without seeing anyone. A crashing noise made them turn to the front. The buck, having observed the hunter, was off like the wind.

The Captain turned round again. The remaining scout was standing with his back to him, his long bow in his left hand, while his profile showed over the right and then over the left shoulder as he searched for his missing comrade. He seemed as puzzled as the Englishman.

Smith was angry. But before he could express his feelings he saw another disturbance among the trees. At first he thought it was another animal—and that the game he was seeking was within reach.

But he was wrong. While he was looking an Indian appeared, coming cautiously toward him. Then another showed on the right of the first, a third on his left, and beyond, many more. A band was approaching the startled Captain, who knew he was in trouble. Opecancanough's party, which had been pursuing him over so long a distance, had caught up with him at last.

The leaders of the Indians were almost as quick to discover their man as he had been to see them. Twenty signals passed among them as the band pressed toward the Captain, who held his ground. It looked to Smith as though there were three hundred of them; there were probably fewer, but there were enough of them to show that little hope remained for him.

If there was any doubt as to their intentions, twenty of the warriors sent their arrows flying among the trees and branches at the white man. Some arrows went wild and clipped off the twigs near him, but two nipped his clothing. He fixed his eye on the foremost Indian, who had come near hitting him with his arrow, and noting that he was fitting a second one to his string, he took careful aim at the warrior and shot him dead.

During these dramatic moments the scout stood as if unable to move or speak. Although he held a fine bow, he made no attempt to use it. It was too much to expect him to assault his own people, when there was no chance of helping the white man by doing so. Captain Smith did not expect him to do this, but his quick wit saw a way in which the scout could help him.

Two steps brought the Captain so near the scout that he could have touched his back. "Stand where you are! Don't move!" commanded Smith, in his most awe-inspiring voice. "They won't shoot through you to reach me."

Smith was bigger than his shield, so he crouched down, peeping from behind the scout at his enemies, who were baffled for the moment. Despite the trying situation, Smith managed to reload his musket, keeping his body shielded by that of his Indian friend. Even though it would have been easy for the scout to break away and join the other Indians, he protected Smith as well as he could. The warriors showed by their actions that they did not want to hurt him. What helped Smith most of all, though, was the dread which the band, large as it was, felt of the powerful weapon that had stretched one of their number lifeless on the ground. Smith had only to turn the muzzle of his gun toward the most daring of his enemies to make them dodge back behind the trees.

The Captain saw that the right course was not to fire until he had to do so to save himself. So long as his attackers knew that their leader was sure to fall they would hold back. How long this would last remained to be seen.

Smith's foes were so numerous that by spreading out they would soon be able to surround him. He could not protect himself from all sides with the scout's body. It seemed that the best thing to do was to surrender before he had increased the Indians' anger by killing more of them.

As Smith attempted to retreat, a warrior, more than six feet tall, his face stained with *puccoon*, and crowned with eagle feathers, had worked so far to the right of the European that the latter could no longer effectively screen himself behind his friend.

The warrior darted from one tree to another, gaining the advantage he was seeking. He stepped from behind the trunk that had sheltered him and carefully aimed at the slowly retreating Smith. Before he could fully draw the arrow, he cried out loudly and fell forward with his long bow bent under him. Smith had fired again—and none too soon.

The unexpected shot checked the warriors for a minute, giving Smith time to reload his weapon. He took a couple of steps back, saying to his scout, "We've got to keep moving until I tell you to stop."

Just then, Smith noticed something startling. One of the Indians had an English musket in his hands! Less than thirty feet away another warrior held a similar gun. Smith knew what it meant. The two friends he had left in camp had been killed. He now had nobody to fall back on.

But even then Smith did not give up. He would continue retreating and fighting until the warriors brought him down. He did not surrender when one of the arrows pierced his thigh, making a slight wound. Then he noticed that the man shielding him had also been hit. The scout's countrymen were growing impatient and were starting to fire their arrows with less care for his safety. His life would not be spared unless Smith stepped aside.

Gallantly, Smith pushed his friend aside so strongly that he had to take many steps to keep from falling. The Captain retreated faster, meaning to hold his fire as long as he could, but ready to use the musket the instant it was needed. He was moving so quickly he could not look where he placed his feet; he put his right foot down, but instead of finding firm support, the leg sank to the knee in soft mud. Smith made a desperate effort to wrench it free, but the left foot went down as far as the other. He struggled but sank farther, until both legs were imbedded in the ooze almost to his thighs.

This brought the end of his resistance. The clinging mud seemed colder than ice. He knew he would die, even if the Indians left him alone. He flung his musket away and threw up his hands.

"I yield! I surrender!" he cried in the Indians' language.

Most of the warriors feared to draw closer—Smith's weapon had filled them with dread. The few with more courage went to the floundering man and grasped his outstretched hands, pulling him onto hard ground.

The Captain knew from experience that these people were unfamiliar with many European inventions. As he asked, in a voice of authority, for their chief, he took hold of a small compass in an ivory case that he carried at his side. Deftly untying the string, he held the little instrument so that all could see the tiny needle flickering back and forth under the glass cover. They crowded around for a better view, not knowing whether to retreat or hold their ground.

Finally, one timidly reached forward and tried to place his finger on the dancing needle. But something stopped it before it touched the restless bit of metal. With a gasp, the warrior recoiled. What had stopped him was the thin covering of glass, which none of the Indians had ever seen before.

The Indian tried to touch the needle again, only to be repulsed as before. He bent his head further over the compass, inspecting the hard substance that stopped him. His head almost touched Smith's chin. Smith noted that, while this Indian was dressed much the same as the others, he had more stained eagle plumes in his long black hair, and he wore a broader and finer sash around his waist. His leggings had numerous ornamental fringes, and there were more beads on his moccasins.

It flashed upon Smith that this warrior was the chief he had asked for a few minutes before—Opecancanough. When the chief straightened up, after he had learned why he could not touch the needle, Smith offered the compass to him. He smiled and shook his head.

By this time, Smith was so cold that his teeth started chattering. His captors kindly rubbed the icy mud from his clothes and led him back to the camp where his dead friends lay. The fire was burning strongly and he was able to warm himself.

After their interest in the compass wore off, the warriors discussed what to do with Smith. Two of them came forward, each taking him by an arm, and led him to a tree, to which he was bound with deer thongs. Then the company formed a circle, and each Indian slowly drew an arrow, with the point leveled at him. Smith closed his eyes and uttered a prayer.

Opecancanough stood a little apart from

the others, and before they could launch the deadly arrows he commanded them in a loud voice to stop. At the same moment he held up the compass that he had taken from the captive. His men promptly lowered their weapons.

Smith became hopeful, though he feared that his death had been merely postponed. His captors would not forgive him since he had slain two of their number—even though the Indians had killed three of the white men.

A line of march was formed with Opecan-canough in the center, the English swords and muskets carried as trophies before him. Next to him walked Smith, his arms held by two warriors, while on either side marched six in single file.

The procession moved through the forest until it reached Orapakes, a hunting home of Powhatan, on the north side of Chickahominy Swamp. This village had about forty mat houses. Women and children swarmed out of the houses and stared in amazement at the prisoner. The warriors began a grand war dance around Smith and Opecancanough. When they had finished dancing, they led Smith to a large matted wigwam, into which he went, while twenty Indians stood guard outside. Smith was unbound and he sat on a bearskin near the entrance to the lodge.

A couple of warriors appeared bearing venison and bread, which they placed before the captive, who was so hungry that he ate his fill. The next morning a sick man was brought to Smith for him to heal. Smith said he could get medicine at Jamestown, but he wasn't allowed to leave.

His captors also asked him to help destroy Jamestown. They promised him all the land and as many wives as he wanted. He assured the Indians that their plan was doomed to fail and that those who tried it would suffer greatly. His words had the right effect, for the plan was given up.

Several weeks followed in which Captain Smith was exhibited through the country, with crowds swarming to look at him as if he were a strange animal. During this troubling time Smith kept looking for Pocahontas or Nantaquas. They must have known of the kindness he had shown the girl. But he saw nothing of either. Finally, Opecancanough brought the captive before the mighty Powhatan himself. There the question of what to do with Smith would be settled.

Chapter 10

Pocahontas Saves Captain Smith

THE SCENE WAS remarkable. The tall, haughty Powhatan sat on a framework suggestive of a throne, covered with mats, in front of a large fire. He was wrapped in a raccoon-skin robe. On each side sat a young woman, two of his wives, and along the sides of the royal lodge stood two rows of men, with the same number of women standing behind them.

As Smith was brought before this imposing company, he knew that the Emperor was about to decide his fate, for the prisoner had been brought there to hear his sentence. As the Captain bowed to Powhatan he looked about for Pocahontas and Nantaquas, and saw the latter. He was standing on the right of the Emperor. His eyes met those of Smith, but there was not the slightest change of expression. Whatever his feelings were, the youth dared give no sign.

But where was Pocahontas? Twice Smith searched among the group, but that gentle, pitying face was not to be seen. The prisoner's heart sank. A woman brought Smith a wooden bowl of water in which he washed his hands. Another woman brought him a bunch of soft feathers to use as a towel. Then came a ceremonial meal for the captive and a long consultation.

Powhatan and his brother chiefs would have spared Smith, but for the fact that he had killed two of their people. That was an offense that could not be pardoned, and so he was sentenced to death. Two warriors entered the lodge, each struggling to carry a heavy stone. The stones were placed together in front of Powhatan.

At a sign from Powhatan six of his men went over to Smith and dragged him and pushed him forward, his hands tied behind his back, and then he was flung to the ground and his head forced down so that it rested on one of the stones. He did not resist, for this man of many adventures felt that the last of them had come.

Most of the warriors fell away, leaving one on either side of the captive. These stood near his shoulders and each held a huge club, the large end swinging clear of the ground, in position for them to draw it back and bring it down on Smith's head with such force that no second blow would be needed.

Intense silence reigned in the lodge. No one

seemed to breathe, and only the rustle of the fire and the moaning of the winter wind outside broke the stillness. All eyes were fixed upon Smith and his executioners. No sign of pity showed on the face of any of them. Powhatan did not give any command or speak, for it was not needed. The two with the clubs knew their duty.

In this tense moment, a movement was heard on the left of the Emperor. It was Pocahontas. With a gasping exclamation, she dashed between the men in front of her, thrusting them out of her way, and, bounding across the intervening space, dropped on one knee, placed an arm on either side of the Captain's head, and with tears streaming down her cheeks, looked up at her father.

"You must not kill him! He is my friend! He was kind to Pocahontas! Spare his life, dear father, for *me!*"

No one moved or spoke. Powhatan glared angrily at his daughter—neither she nor anyone else had ever dared to do a thing like this before. Had it been anyone else, he would have struck the person dead at his feet.

But he could not raise a hand against his beloved daughter. He started to rise, but changed his mind and sank back down again. The executioners looked at him, awaiting his

"You must not kill him! He is my friend! He was kind
to Pocahontas! Spare his life, dear father, for *me!*"

command and paying no attention to the girl kneeling between them, with her arms still around Captain Smith's neck. He looked up into her dark, pitying eyes and a warm tear fell on his bronzed forehead. With one hand Pocahontas brushed back the heavy brown hair that had dropped over his eyes, and smiling through her grief, said:

"You shall not be harmed! Your life is spared!"

"How can you know that, my good friend?"

"Don't you see?" she asked, trying to help him to his feet.

The warriors with their huge clubs had stepped away from the two. Powhatan could not deny the prayer of Pocahontas, and had signaled them to spare the life of the Englishman.

When Smith stood up, his face went red with embarrassment. Not knowing what to do, he stood staring at the ground. Pocahontas fluttered around him like a bird. She tried to untie the knots that bound his wrists behind his back, and though she would have succeeded in a few minutes, she was impatient. She beckoned to her brother, Nantaquas, who came quickly forward and cut the thongs with his knife. He turned inquiringly to Powhatan, who motioned for his son to take the man away. Taking the hand of the prisoner in his own, the youth led him out of the wigwam. Pocahontas did not follow, but did another thing that astonished the group. Forgetful of all his royal dignity, she bounded to the throne, flung her arms around her father's neck and sobbed with thankfulness, murmuring words only Powhatan could hear.

For the moment, the great chieftain forgot that he was Emperor. He stroked his daughter's hair until she regained command of herself. He told her that he had spared the prisoner because he could deny nothing to her. Her face glowed, tears still shining, as she walked back to where she was before.

Meanwhile, Nantaquas took Smith to his own lodge at the eastern edge of the village. It was only a dozen feet in length and about eight feet wide, with a fire at one end, and animal skins and furs on the floor and walls.

The Indian youth had learned the Englishmen's custom of greeting one another by shaking hands. When the Captain, therefore, offered his hand to his friend, it was promptly grasped by him.

"I shall always be grateful to you, Nantaquas."

"Your thanks belong to my sister," was the gentle reply.

"I know that, and she will dwell ever in my heart. Does this mean that my life is spared for a short time only?"

"I will learn. Wait till I come back."

The Indian youth slipped outside. Captain Smith sat down on one of the furs and thought over the strange things that had happened. He was still thinking when his friend returned.

Nantaquas had talked with Powhatan, who told him that Smith was to stay among the Indians, and give his time to making moccasins, bows and arrows, and especially beads, bells and copper trinkets for Pocahontas. The Captain accepted the proposal with great pleasure, for he knew that sooner or later he would return to Jamestown.

What a contrast between the stormy scenes he had passed through and this quiet working in the depths of the American woods! He took up the task with the same energy he put into everything, and pleased Nantaquas, who showed a real friendship for him. Powhatan was also quite satisfied, and Pocahontas, who often came to the little workshop and watched the sturdy Captain at work, was delighted. She would sometimes sit for hours at a time on a mat in front of him, noting with great interest the movements of the skillful fingers that worked so deftly, though they were more used to handling a sword than to making delicate ornaments and trinkets. She could not restrain her happiness as the articles gradually took form. When the Captain finished a pair of moccasins that were as dainty as Cinderella's slippers, she slipped them on her feet, clapped her hands and danced about the wigwam. Nantaquas and Captain Smith smiled at the pretty picture and the brave and good Captain felt well rewarded for his efforts. Indeed, could he ever repay this sweet daughter of the forest for what she had done for him? He often asked himself the question, and the answer was always a soft, but heartfelt, "No!"

Powhatan left no doubt of his friendly feelings toward Captain Smith when, six weeks after he had started on his voyage up the Chickahominy, the chieftain allowed him to return under guard to Jamestown. He received a warm welcome from his countrymen, and the Indians who had come with him were sent back with many presents for themselves, and still more for the grand Emperor himself.

Chapter 11

Pocahontas Saves the Colony

BRIEF AS SMITH'S absence had been, the settlement had reached the brink of ruin. Hard times had come to Jamestown. The poor people, besides quarreling among themselves, began starving to death. The thin, famished settlers staggered along the single street, too feeble to rise when they stumbled and fell. All they could do was creep into their cabins and wait for death. It looked as if no one would be left alive; the only one who kept on his feet and moved about was Captain Smith. He was always hopeful and helped others with his unfailing good spirits.

But the day came when even Smith began to give up hope. He did not know where to get the next mouthful of food without going to the Indians, and his companions were too weak to go with him. He would not leave them to their fate, but was ready to die with them.

Standing gloomily on the outside of the palisades, with arms folded and looking off along the trail that led to the forest, he suddenly saw a strange sight. A girl came out from among the trees, bearing a basket of corn on her shoulder. He had hardly time to recognize her as Pocahontas, when he saw she was followed by other Indians. He counted eighteen in the procession. The one next to her was Nantaquas, and, filing after him, were other warriors, every one carrying a basket of corn or a haunch of venison. Their hearts were moved with pity for the perishing Europeans. If not for this kindness, all the settlers would have died.

The grateful Englishmen referred to this good maiden ever after as "the dear and blessed Pocahontas." She came once or twice a week for months, bringing supplies through the woods to Jamestown. She had convinced Powhatan that it would be best for everyone if the Indians helped the white men. And even though there was often fighting between the two peoples, Pocahontas never weakened in her friendship to the colonists.

Sometimes Pocahontas's father became angry with her, and though parent and child did not quarrel, the girl became more guarded in her deeds of kindness when Powhatan was at war with the Englishmen.

During one of these wars, Smith set out one

A girl came out from among the trees, bearing a
basket of corn on her shoulder.

day with a strong company to surprise Powhatan. He had not been gone long when nine of those he had left at home went out in a boat in a severe storm. The boat turned over and the men were drowned. Since Smith was counting on these men as backup, it was important that he be told of the accident.

The task of reaching Smith through the many miles of wilderness was so dangerous that only one man in the colony was willing to go. During his journey, he was captured by the Indians and taken before Powhatan. The chieftain ordered him to be put to death. Without drawing suspicion to herself, Pocahontas got him a short distance away in the woods and hid him among the bushes. He would have been found and brought back by the warriors who set out to look for him had she not led them in the wrong direction. The man gained enough of a start to join Smith and tell him what had happened to the men he had been counting on for help.

Some time later, when matters seemed to have quieted down, a party of colonists went among Powhatan's people to trade. However, all except one man were massacred. Pocahontas succeeded in saving his life, and he lived among the Indians for many years, secure in her friendship.

Without drawing suspicion to herself, Pocahontas got him a short distance away in the woods and hid him among the bushes.

Chapter 12

Pocahontas Is Married

THREE YEARS AFTER Captain Smith and his fellow settlers had arrived in the land of Powhatan, Smith returned to England. He never came back, and after his departure, the settlement suffered even greater losses. When Smith left, there were five hundred men in Jamestown; only sixty were alive at the end of six months.

Gradually, though, conditions improved and more and more people came from England to settle in the colony. Many of these people tried to take advantage of the Native Americans, and even Pocahontas, who had always acted on behalf of the colonists, was not safe when there was fighting between the English and the Indians.

One of the English Captains, Samuel Argall, was an explorer and adventurer like Captain Smith. Early in 1613, while leading an expedition up the Potomac River to find food for the settlers, he met Pocahontas and another Indian woman who sometimes accompanied her on her walks. Pocahontas, though she was a young woman now, still looked much the same as when Smith first saw her in the canoe with Nantaquas. She still held a great affection for the English and did not hesitate when Captain Argall invited her to visit his ship. Suspecting no evil, Pocahontas came aboard with her companion. Unknown to the Indian Princess, however, the woman had been bribed with Argall's promise that no harm would come to Pocahontas. When her companion went back ashore, Pocahontas was kept a prisoner. Argall's expectation was that Powhatan would be glad to pay a huge ransom in corn for her return to him. But instead of doing so, the chieftain prepared to wage an even fiercer war against the colony.

During these troubling weeks Pocahontas stayed at Jamestown, where everyone treated her kindly. At this time, Pocahontas learned more about the English people's way of life and their religion. Taking their beliefs to heart, she converted to Christianity. At her baptism she was given an English name, Rebecca. One of the colonists, John Rolfe, became interested in the maiden, and she returned his affection.

Rolfe and Pocahontas were married in April 1613. Although Powhatan did not attend the ceremony, he cheerfully gave his consent and sent his brother and two of his sons to repre-

When her companion went back ashore, Pocahontas
was kept a prisoner.

sent him. One of them was Nantaquas, who was very pleased with the marriage. Pocahontas' uncle gave her away in accordance with Anglican ritual. The windows were decorated with evergreens, wildflowers and crimson berries. The settlers and Indians crowded the small building, gazing upon the beautiful scene.

The bride was dressed in a simple tunic of white muslin, her arms bared to the shoulders. She had a rich robe that she had embroidered herself. Her black hair flowed down her back and a fillet filled with bright plumage held a cloudlike veil.

Rolfe was dressed like an English cavalier, with a short sword on his thigh. The clergyman, with impressive voice and manner, amid the breathless hush of the spectators, made the two man and wife.

The marriage was happy in all ways. Husband and wife devotedly loved each other, and Powhatan became the true friend of the English, and remained so to the end of his life. When the English Governor, Sir Thomas Dale, sailed for England in 1616, he took Rolfe and Pocahontas, or "Lady Rebecca," with him. She received a great deal of attention from the royal court, and was well-loved by the people she met. Everyone was anxious to make her happy in this new and strange land.

Pocahontas was anxious to meet her old friend, John Smith. He was the first person she asked about. But, to her grief, she was told that he was dead. While she was in mourning for him, Captain Smith came to see her. She was so shocked that she burst into tears.

She soon regained her cheerfulness and the two sat down and had a long talk over their lives in America, three thousand miles away. She called the Captain "father," and he returned the honor by calling her "daughter."

Rolfe and his wife were preparing to sail back to America when she fell ill at Gravesend and died at the age of twenty-one. Her infant son, Thomas, was taken to London and educated by his uncle, Henry Rolfe. When he reached adulthood he sailed to America, back to the land that was his mother's home.

DOVER
CHILDREN'S THRIFT CLASSICS

Just $1.00
All books complete and unabridged, except where noted.
96pp., 5³/₁₆" × 8¼", paperbound.

AESOP'S FABLES, Aesop. 28020-9

THE LITTLE MERMAID AND OTHER FAIRY TALES, Hans Christian Andersen. 27816-6

THE UGLY DUCKLING AND OTHER FAIRY TALES, Hans Christian Andersen. 27081-5

THE THREE BILLY GOATS GRUFF AND OTHER READ-ALOUD STORIES, Carolyn Sherwin Bailey (ed.). 28021-7

THE STORY OF PETER PAN, James M. Barrie and Daniel O'Connor. 27294-X

ROBIN HOOD, Bob Blaisdell. 27573-6

THE ADVENTURES OF BUSTER BEAR, Thornton W. Burgess. 27564-7

THE ADVENTURES OF CHATTERER THE RED SQUIRREL, Thornton W. Burgess. 27399-7

THE ADVENTURES OF DANNY MEADOW MOUSE, Thornton W. Burgess. 27565-5

THE ADVENTURES OF GRANDFATHER FROG, Thornton W. Burgess. 27400-4

THE ADVENTURES OF JERRY MUSKRAT, Thornton W. Burgess. 27817-4

THE ADVENTURES OF JIMMY SKUNK, Thornton W. Burgess. 28023-3

THE ADVENTURES OF PETER COTTONTAIL, Thornton W. Burgess. 26929-9

THE ADVENTURES OF POOR MRS. QUACK, Thornton W. Burgess. 27818-2

THE ADVENTURES OF REDDY FOX, Thornton W. Burgess. 26930-2

THE SECRET GARDEN, Frances Hodgson Burnett. (abridged) 28024-1

PICTURE FOLK-TALES, Valery Carrick. 27083-1

THE STORY OF POCAHONTAS, Brian Doherty (ed.). 28025-X

SLEEPING BEAUTY AND OTHER FAIRY TALES, Jacob and Wilhelm Grimm. 27084-X

THE ELEPHANT'S CHILD AND OTHER JUST SO STORIES, Rudyard Kipling. 27821-2

HOW THE LEOPARD GOT HIS SPOTS AND OTHER JUST SO STORIES, Rudyard Kipling. 27297-4

MOWGLI STORIES FROM "THE JUNGLE BOOK," Rudyard Kipling. 28030-6

NONSENSE POEMS, Edward Lear. 28031-4

BEAUTY AND THE BEAST AND OTHER FAIRY TALES, Marie Leprince de Beaumont and Charles Perrault. 28032-2

A DOG OF FLANDERS, Ouida (Marie Louise de la Ramée). 27087-4

PETER RABBIT AND 11 OTHER FAVORITE TALES, Beatrix Potter. 27845-X